WARNING

This book contains sexually explicit scenes and adult language. It may be considered offensive to some readers. This book is for sale to adults ONLY.

* * * * * * * * * * * * * * * * * *

Please store your files wisely where they cannot be accessed by underage readers.

ISBN-13: 978-1987863987
ISBN-10: 1987863984

Other Books by Darla Dunbar:

<u>The Romeo Alpha BBW Paranormal Shifter Romance Series</u>

Amanda Walker thinks that she has a normal and boring life. That is until after her 24th birthday. Everything changes when she meets the man who says he was supposed to be her husband. Denying everything the man says, she fights him every step of the way. But after he kidnaps her, Amanda discovers that there are some things about her family that her parents kept a secret all these years. Among the history of the family she learns secrets she thought only happened in story books. Can Amanda tell the difference between truth and lies or is she this mysterious woman that holds the key to a legacy?

<u>Romeo Alpha Blood Lines Romance Series</u>

Twenty-four years have passed in relative peace for Amanda and Romeo. They've raised five children into adulthood and are thoroughly enjoying their lives as the Alpha King and Queen of the werewolves. At twenty-four, Sarina is just stepping into her powers and will be ripe for mating when her birthday comes in two weeks. What no one knows is the danger that lurks just outside their tight knit community. Romeo has made peace with the other clans and has enjoyed that peace, but it will all come crashing down around him when his oldest daughter comes of age to take a mate.

The Alpha Feud BBW Paranormal Shifter Romance Series

Eliza's life consisted of reporting on boring, crowd-pleasing events, like their country livestock fair. With the arrival of two handsome brothers, the lives of Eliza and her best friend, Melissa, are shaken to the core. For Eliza, the arrival of this new man becomes a test of her relationship with her current boyfriend, who she's been happily living with for over six years. Does Hayden, a complete stranger, really wield the power to make Eliza reconsider her relationship with Andrew?

The Alpha Packed BBW Paranormal Shifter Romance Series

Darlene has led a quiet life since suffering through a terrible break-up. She wants nothing more than to spend her time in front of the TV, away from any sort of trouble. But all that goes down the drain when handsome, rugged and rough Idris comes into her life. He is a werewolf on the lookout for his missing pack leader. Darlene quickly finds herself pulled towards this mysterious man and at the same time finds herself falling deeper and deeper into the world of the supernatural.

The Daemon Paranormal Romance Chronicles

The daemon infighting can only be stopped when a strong leader emerges to calm the different factions. Juno appears to be at the heart of the conflict. Things become complicated when Phoebe and Supay try to negotiate with the siren, Juno. The love triangle among Phoebe, Supay and Apollo become tense when Juno's meddling threatens to destroy any romance that develops.

<u>The Leather Satchel Paranormal Romance Series</u>

Valtina is stuck in Middle World, unable to pass on to The Afterlife. In order to redeem herself from past deeds done, she must help bring romance back into the world and stop The Dark Side from destroying love in its entirety. Following orders issued by Ladaya and armed with a leather satchel filled with the appropriate tools and weapons, Valtina embraces each mission with enthusiasm.

Get the latest update on new releases from the author at:

https://darladunbar.com/newsletter/

This book is Part Three of the "The Mind Talker Paranormal Romance Series"

Book 1 - Awareness

Ananda discovered that she can read other people's mind when she was 11. It is supposed to be a gift but it's driving her crazy. Lonely and disoriented, Ananda runs off to New York. She thinks that in a city as big as that, there must be someone like her walking around. One day, man's voice calls out to her. The strange thing is that she heard the voice in her mind.

Book 2 - Hunted

Jared's past haunted him and served as a reminder that he can't escape his fate. If he had stopped the boy back then, would his sister still be alive? Jenny was the love of Jared's life until he discovered she was living a double life. Jenny was part of a secret organization that was bent on hunting him.

Book 3 - Heat

Ananda couldn't help herself. Jared's scent just sends her over the edge. No one else understood Ananda's gift... not even her parents. When Jared found Ananda, he explained what her special powers meant. Only certain people acquired the gift of reading minds. Along with that, Ananda was undergoing a maturation process. Every one of her kind will experience it in their 21st year.

Book 4 - Revealed

Jared learns the truth about his dead sister. Ananda had
the power to see into his past. She saw what he saw
during that fateful day when Jared's sister died.
Meanwhile, the truth about Kerri's family is revealed.
They are the sole reason why Ananda and her kind are
on the endangered list.

Book 5 - Evasion

Ryan is the mystery man who is helping Jared and
Ananda to escape to Canada in hopes of evading the
organization that is hunting all those with special mind
reading powers. Kerri's family is behind the secret
organization. Her love for Ryan has forced her to
choose between loyalty to family and loyalty to Ryan.
Can she be trusted?

The Mind Talker Paranormal Romance Series

Heat

Book Three

By Darla Dunbar

Table of Contents

Chapter One.. 1
Chapter Two 7
Chapter Three 12
Chapter Four.. 17
Other Books by Darla Dunbar.............................. 37
About the Author - Darla Dunbar 38
Connect with Darla Dunbar................................. 39

Chapter One

TYPICALLY, on a normal day, Ananda woke up securely warm and cocooned in the down-filled blankets of her bed. The window over her bed had no blinds, only sheer curtains that fully allowed the rising sun to shine brightly, illuminating the room and waking her gradually. What she did not normally wake up to is her skin overwrought with sensitive nerves, itchiness demanding her attention, and skin feeling one degree away from boiling. Slitting her eyes open, Ananda could see moonlight seeping through a crack in curtains that absolutely did not belong to her, creating random shadow patterns on the wall that did nothing to calm the frantic beating of her heart. If not for the familiar arm stretched out around her waist, she would have jerked out of bed. As it was she simply gazed around while letting her mind catch up to the situation.

Shifting slightly, Ananda was unpleasantly surprised when a bolt of pain shot down her spine. "Ow ow, fuck ow! What the hell did you do to me?!"

"…Nothing that you didn't ask for."

The unexpected answer pushed a small huff of laughter between Ananda's lips until her breath was coming out in wheezing gasps. She could feel herself beginning to panic and who could blame her? Her skin felt like it was on fire, she was in bed with a man she met barely a day ago and she was running from some unknown entity that broke into the house she shared with a best friend who she was afraid she'd either never see again or would only hear about on the news. All things considered, panicking was the tamest thing she could be doing at this point when compared to the alternatives such as running screaming into oncoming traffic.

Ananda considered calling her parents and then quickly pushed that thought from her mind. All she needed was for them to once again think that she was crazy when she explained about hearing other people's voices and apparently finding someone who shared that same gift. Not to mention having to explain to them that she was currently shacked up with said person in a slightly sleazy hotel room after having explosive sex that left her catatonic for…

"How long have I been out?" Ananda would have been surprised by the breathy quality of her voice if she weren't still trying to gain control of her body and regulate her breathing. The hand that had been resting on her stomach was now moving softly in a circle that, amazingly, was helping her regain her sense of calm. That musky, citrusy scent was back and curling softly about her, somehow cooling the heat that settled right underneath her skin. She could feel the aches from their previous bedroom activities diminishing until all she felt was a dull buzz. "God that's like catnip or something…" Her voice trailed off into a satisfied gasp. The hand on her stomach paused for a moment but once again continued after she whimpered softly.

"You've only been asleep for maybe an hour," Jared's deep voice rumbled. Ananda could feel the vibrations travel down her back and she shifted back into the man's warmth more fully until she could hardly tell where he began and she ended. She once again thought about calling someone, particularly Kerri, at least to check and see if her friend was okay. Then again, she knew that if she called then her friend would without a doubt come to wherever the hell they were without a second's hesitation. Ananda wasn't too keen on having her friend burst in while she was still in the thralls of whatever heat wave her body had decided to fling itself into.

So she relaxed back into Jared's stable arms once again closing her eyes and relaxing into the silence. Strangely she felt no need to talk or fill the room with any sound other than their soft breaths. Despite the abrupt situation that she somehow landed in, Ananda felt more comfortable with Jared than she ever had with anyone else. She could feel his thoughts slowly unfurling and yet she felt no need to push to read into them more clearly. It wasn't that she was uninterested, more that she felt he would let her in on them when needed. Until then she was content to leave him to his own private musings while taking whatever comfort he was willing to give her. The fire that had burned bright under her skin had tempered itself and though she still felt a bit antsy, overall it was manageable.

Ananda fell back into a slight doze, waking slightly when she felt the arm slide away from her waist and the bed shift with motion.

"Jared?" She intoned sleepily, turning slightly in order to peer at the man over her shoulder. Her body no longer ached and instead she felt almost energized, a warm buzz of contentment just under skin. She caught a glimpse of the man's broad muscular back before the form turned and she was looking up into those amazingly blue eyes that seemed to glow with some unnamed emotion always present right underneath the surface. Jared peered down at her for a few moments before he leaned over to kiss Ananda deeply. She reached up to card her fingers through the rasp of his stubble enjoying the scratchiness against the skin of her fingertips. When he pulled back there was a ghost of a smile lingering on the man's lips and Ananda settled back into the pillow with a small smile of her own. Somehow she knew that it was imperative to get as much sleep as possible for now and so she closed her eyes as Jared moved to the bathroom shutting the door softly behind him.

The next time Ananda woke up was less than pleasant. The agonizing itchiness was back as was the molten fire burning underneath her skin. She made a short relieved sound as she scratched her nails down the skin of her arm, a choked noise escaping her throat as she attempted and failed to quell the sensation of her skin burning from the inside out. Ananda's back arched as a sharp sensation of arousal flared from deep inside of her.

"What the hell…" she panted. Never before had she felt such a strong sensation. Truly looking around for the first time, Ananda realized with dismay that she was alone in the hotel room. Glancing at the side table, she saw a phone with a note stuck to it. Without thinking she grabbed it, dialing the number that Jared left for her to use. With every unanswered ring, Ananda could feel her mind growing more and more alarmed, the panic that had been earlier pushed back threatening to make a reappearance.

"Yeah?" Jared finally answered, annoyance clear in his voice. It took a few tries before Ananda could push back the panic in order to get her voice to work.

"Jared…" she moaned as another jolt of arousal nearly made her double over. "Something's wrong. I feel so hot." Her voice trailed off in another moan as the blanket scraped over her now engorged nipples. Looking down she could see that they were slightly swollen and red with need. Without thinking she trailed one hand up until she could graze the pad of her finger over the sensitive nub. The feeling that shot up her chest was amazing and her panting grew harsher as she forgot why the sensation was unwanted. Dimly she could hear a crash and a shrill curse on the other end of the line, followed by muffled voices and quickly moving footsteps. It wasn't until she heard the slam of a car door that Ananda jerked her hand away from her chest and refocused on the man on the other end of the phone.

"Ananda, listen to me carefully," Jared spoke quietly yet intensely. Ananda could hear the sound of an engine being started up and the squealing of tires. "Do not go near any of the windows or door. Stay in the bed, and try to stay as quiet as you can."

Nodding and trying not to be alarmed, Ananda once again trailed a hand to her chest, kneading one breast with a groan before turning to do the same to the other. The fact that she could hear Jared cursing softly over the phone seemed to rile her up even more.

"Are you touching yourself Ananda?" Jared growled, his voice as deep as thunder. It sent a tingle down Ananda's spine and she wished that the man was the one touching her. "Are you feeling your greedy little body? Is your skin hot baby? You want me to be the one touching you don't you?"

"Yes," she hissed, fingers skirting down her flat stomach until they slowly crawled through the dark hair that framed her hidden warmth. "Touching myself and I don't know why. Why is my body so hot? Why do I feel like I'll die without you touching me?" Ananda's fingers reached down further until she found herself drenched with slick and almost unbearably sensitive to the touch. Despite Jared's admonishment to stay as quiet as possible, Ananda couldn't help the needy grunts and groans that escaped as she slipped two fingers into her pulsing channel. She was so slick that there was no discomfort, only a feeling of 'yes.'

"Ananda," Jared growled. She had forgotten that she still had him on the phone, so caught up in the demands of her body.

Whining, Ananda tried to focus. "Tell me. Why do I feel this way? Please…"

Chapter Two

The sound of screeching tires sounded almost too loud to be coming from the phone and Ananda jerked when she heard the door to the room being flung open until it crashed against the wall. Seeing Jared standing in the doorway, eyes wild and chest heaving was the missing piece, and Ananda found herself flung head-first into a powerful orgasm. When she came back she was once again gathered in Jared's strong arms as the man slowly caressed her damp cheek.

"You're in, well I guess the easiest way to explain is to say you're in heat. It's something we all go through in our twenty-first year. Our bodies are going through the last maturation stage which is full sexual maturity." Jared's voice wavered slightly as Ananda began to slowly writhe, succumbing to the throes of passion once again. She turned watery eyes upward to gaze at the man and swallowed as his nostrils flared, eyes dilated until there was only a small ring of blue left.

"Jared," she whined, frantically reaching to pull the man down to her lips. Though the heat had quieted slightly with his soft touch against her cheek it just wasn't enough and she desperately needed to feel his heated body against her own. She could feel his body hardening underneath her back and she wondered why he didn't just take what they both wanted.

"Because I want you to be sure," Jared answered, fingers carding through her hair as he sent calming thoughts through their already forming bond. He shifted their bodies around until he was reclining slightly with Ananda resting between his outstretched legs. He slowly and carefully began massaging her shoulders and arms, transferring his feelings of calm to his fingertips and willing her heat to recede. Though her scent was incredibly enticing, he was being truthful when he said he wanted her to be sure before things went further between them. He wouldn't be like Jenny, he wouldn't treat Ananda as disposable. Nor could he place the burden on her of being matched with him for a lifetime before she truly got the chance to live and experience life.

As if sensing Jared's inner musings, Ananda curled her hand into his squeezing in what she hoped was understood reassurance. "I get it Jared. I really do. I'm being ruled by my emotions, pulled along by my maturing libido, blah blah blah." She tried to take a calming breath and get her thoughts in order. "The thing is…you smell really good to me, and you feel really good to me. Now, I might not completely know what that means, but the fact that in all of the people I've ever slept with, not once has it all hit me like that at once."

A low humming growl filled the air as Jared's chest rumbled soothingly against Ananda's back relaxing her even further.

"You smell good to me too," Jared whispered, nose sliding up the sensitive skin behind her ear as he took in more of her scent in deep controlled breaths. "But you should know everything about us before you do something and later regret it."

"But I want you so bad," Ananda whined, turning swiftly to face his lips, meeting in a kiss that she swore she could feel deep in her core. Deep down Ananda knew this man. She knew Jared; his story, his life, his very essence called to her in a way that could never be matched by another human being. His protests and inclination to create space between them was completely unacceptable and she knew that even while he pulled away, it wasn't what he truly wanted.

Jared was trying so hard to do the noble thing, turn Ananda away until she was lucid enough to really think about the possible ramifications of their actions. Already a bond was building between them that would be a pain to sever, but if they didn't stop now, if they allowed it to continue and strengthen it would be damn near impossible to reverse without serious complications to one or both of them. He didn't want to; God knows he didn't. Everything in him was screaming to cement their connection, to bury himself so far in her that even those with no abilities would somehow be able to sense that they belonged to one another. It was this part of himself that deepened their kiss, making him shift until he was prone against the bed, Ananda's quickly reheating body straddling his hips and pushing her molten core against his hardened shaft. It took everything within him to hold her still when all he really wanted to do was unzip his jeans and once again lose himself in her silky depths.

"Trust me when I say," he panted, pulling away from her sinfully reddened lips. "I want to destroy you with my cock." Unable to help himself, he dove in again, easily prodding her lips apart in order to taste her warmth. "I want to carve a spot so deep inside you that no one but me could ever fill it." The sound of her heated whimper made his rigid prick pulse with want, and almost without thinking he deftly unzipped his pants, pulling himself out and shuddering at his sensitivity.

"Do it Jared, please. I need you and I know you need me." Ananda shifted lower until she could feel the head of Jared's heated shaft lined up against her folds. If not for the man's hesitation she would have plunged herself downward taking all of him into her core. But she could feel the need for him to choose her as if her body would not be satisfied unless a clear decision was made either way. "I need a mate, Jared, my other half. I've been looking for him for so long and now I know…" she trailed off, gasping as one of his hands dug into the meat of her rear.

Jared could feel himself slipping. "You know what?" he hissed, taking Ananda's bottom lip between his teeth and pulling back with a groan. "Tell me what you know. Tell me what you need."

He could feel it; they were poised on a precipice, waiting for that one word…

Opening her eyes, Ananda smiled softly before leaning to rest her lips against his.

"You."

As if hit by a bolt of lightning, Jared's body tightened before plunging into the warm abyss of the woman above. The sound of Ananda's wail of triumph spurred a symphony of growls from Jared as his body sought to fulfill his partner's needs. The air was saturated with the scent of honey and citrus as their pheromones co-mingled and merged, signifying the meshing of souls. The sound of skin meeting skin was deafening as their bodies surged against one another, racing steadily towards the finish line of their climax. Open mouths met as uneven breaths were shared back and forth, neither party able to turn it into a true kiss. With a final snap of his hips, Jared was flung into an orgasm so powerful he swore he'd gone blind. The feeling of warmth surging through her lower body made Ananda clench as her body was hurled over the precipice and into ecstasy while once again everything went black.

Chapter Three

Kerri slowly entered the apartment, dropping her keys onto the table by the door just like she had done countless times before. She knew that it would be empty, Ananda having been taken somewhere else by the stranger who had been tailing them for weeks. It was good that he had come just in time to spirit her friend away, promising to keep the other girl safe from everyone, including herself. It had been an issue that Kerri didn't know quite know how to handle, keeping Ananda safe from the organization that wanted to eradicate people like her, the very same organization that Kerri's father owned. The young woman had known as soon as she met Ananda that she needed to find a way to keep her off of her father's radar, and had been secretly making a plan for months until she realized another person had taken interest in the auburn-haired beauty.

"Hello cousin."

Sighing with annoyance, Kerri turned to the living room to see Jenny sitting casually on the couch as if it were something she did every day. While she could see her cousin smiling, the sentiment never quite reached her eyes, which stayed as cold and blank as one would expect from a killer.

"What are you doing here Jenny? I told my father I wanted nothing to do with his mindless quest for world domination or whatever." Disinterested, Kerri walked into the kitchen noting that the other woman followed her without prompting. She snorted as she pictured a fluffy little Pomeranian with sharp teeth which perfectly fit what she thought of her cousin. Truthfully, Kerri cared little for any of the members of her so-called family. Other than the blood pumping through her veins she had little in common with them and actively tried to distance herself in every way possible. If not for her gift of shielding her thoughts and the thoughts of others, she could pretend that she had come from another family and had simply been adopted at birth. In her mind that would have been preferable to being born into what she saw as a fucked up underground system consisting of her family and those that they routinely tried to either convince to work for them or eradicated.

"Oh I'm not here for you my little basket case," Jenny smirked as she lifted an apple from the table. She inspected the fruit carefully before taking a bite and chewing thoughtfully. "No, I'm here to see your roommate. You know, the one you said was just another normal human, boring and clueless." Turning wicked blue eyes to survey the woman in front of her, Jenny took another bite of the apple before a dangerous glint appeared in her eye. "Turns out she may not be as clueless or boring as you'd originally reported."

Kerri shrugged, trying to appear nonchalant and uncaring about the subject. "I don't know nor do I care what you're talking about. My roommate, as you can see, isn't here. You probably scared her off by, oh I don't know, breaking into our apartment!" The last part was said with barely disguised anger. Kerri had tried so hard to protect Ananda from being discovered and yet she had the worst feeling that her protectiveness may have been what led her family right to her. Trying her damndest to stay calm, Kerri finished her glass of water and carefully placed the cup in the sink before turning once again to face her cousin.

"Look, I told my father I wanted no part in his mindless quest to subdue and coerce innocent people into going along with his machinations. He agreed to leave me alone indefinitely, so why the fuck did I come home to find you in my house, looking for my roommate and disrupting my goddamn life?"

"I interrupted your life?" Jenny's eyes narrowed as she took a step closer to the seething red head. "Wake up princess. This isn't a life, it's a lie. You lie to yourself every day that you wake up and pretend to be just a normal human girl. You're not. Get over it and get with the fucking program." Jenny removed a dagger from her pocket and slammed it on the kitchen counter. Kerri could see it was the ceremonial dagger her father had given to her when she reached 13, the age all children were tested to see if they were gifted. She had abandoned it when she moved out of the family home and excommunicated herself from the others. "You knew that your roommate was one of them; a danger to everyone around her and yet you allowed her to go around undetected. You were willing to risk the lives of others in order to feed some bullshit rebellion against your family."

"I did no such thing!" Kerri screeched, hands balling into fists as her emotions got the best of her.

"Think about how many people could have been hurt or killed if that thing had lost control!"

"Ananda isn't like that!"

"She's a killer!"

"She's my friend!" Kerri screamed, hands coming up and burying themselves in the collar of Jenny's shirt. "She would never hurt anyone and I know it. You all are just too stupid and ruled by fear to stop and think about all of the lives you've ruined with this pointless crusade!" Gathering her strength, Kerri lashed out pushing her cousin away from her. She looked away from the other woman as hot tears threatened to fall from her burning eyes. "Get out."

Jenny gathered herself from the floor, eyes still locked on the petite redhead. "Your feelings cloud your judgment cousin. One day Ananda will lose control, and when she does it will be forever etched on your conscience. I hope you're ready to deal with that."

Turning back to her cousin, Kerri's eyes were blank as she closed off her mind. "Leave my house and never return. I want nothing to do with any of you. And you can tell the man I used to call father, the next time he sends one of you to follow me or do harm to Ananda in any way, I'll return you myself, in a body bag. Have I made myself clear?"

"…Crystal," Jenny answered, turning on her heel and heading towards the door.

Kerri stood in the kitchen, long after the door had been closed, mind rolling with half-formed thoughts. It took her many hours to find sleep that night.

Chapter Four

The next morning, Ananda woke up again with a heavy arm draped around her waist, but this time her body was back to a normal temperature. She did ache slightly, but smiled as the images from last night played again in her mind. Frantic sex had gradually given way to slow and sensual love making as Jared took his time and showed her all of the things she had been missing from her previous partners. Slowly untangling her limbs from the still snoozing man's, she walked into the bathroom and started a warm bath that would help soothe her aching muscles. Ananda gazed at her image in the mirror, hand coming up to touch the dark bruise at the base of her neck that was evidence from the past evening's events. It made her preen inside to carry the mark from Jared and she wanted to show it off to the world to that she had been claimed by him. Her golden eyes almost seemed to glow with happiness. She stepped into the steaming water, groaning at the feeling of warmth and adding a few drops of lavender oil to the bath water. The scent went a long way towards helping relax her and she leaned her head back relaxing further into the tub.

Ananda wasn't sure how long she sat there letting the warmth from the water creep into her weary muscles but she soon became aware of noises coming from the room. Thinking that Jared had finally woken up, she called out to him.

"Hey, come join me in the bath! I found some lavender oil that is really…" Her sentence was cut off as a dark figure hurled itself into the bathroom covering her mouth with its hand and trapping her startled scream. Ananda struggled, limbs flailing and water pouring out of the tub as the figure began calling her name frantically.

"Ananda!"

Ananda shot up out of bed, breath coming in harsh pants as she struggled to make sense of what was happening. Quickly she became aware of her surroundings and found herself sitting in bed, Jared holding her shoulders with panic clear on his face. "What happened?" Ananda asked. It didn't make any sense. Wasn't she in the bath?

"You started yelling in your sleep like someone was trying to kill you. What happened? What did you see?" Jared questioned frantically confusing the woman even more.

"What do you mean what did I see? Aren't I supposed to be able to influence people?" Ananda was confused and growing more alarmed as Jared stood up and began to quickly circle the room packing up what little supplies they had brought with them. He collected their food from the floor, throwing Ananda her clothes and motioning for her to quickly get dressed.

"Not everyone has the same gift. We're all born with the ability to read other's minds and somewhat sense emotions, but once we turn of age sometimes we gain a new gift and that could be anything from being able to influence others to starting fires with our minds. It's why people hunt us down to either capture us or kill us." Finally dressed, Jared grabbed his bag before hustling Ananda out of the room and back into the car. His eyes darted back and forth taking everything in as they pulled out of the parking lot and back on the road. Ananda was quiet as she took in everything that she had learned so far. Finding out that she might somehow have gained the ability to see the future was almost too fantastical to believe.

"So I can see the future. God, how much more of a freak could I possibly be!" Ananda was incensed. She felt herself relax when Jared's hand reached over and covered her own where she had slowly been tightly squeezing her thigh.

"Ananda, no matter what anyone says, you are not a freak. There's nothing wrong with either of us and don't let anyone tell you otherwise." The man's conviction went far to reassure Ananda that although she might be going through some changes, deep down inside she hadn't really changed. She was still her.

"So what happened? Why was someone in my apartment and why are we still running?" Now that Ananda calmed down, she was back to focusing on their first meeting and why Jared was even in the alley in the first place. "And what happened with Kerri?"

Taking his time to gather his thoughts, Jared tightened his hands on the steering wheel, eyes staring straight ahead. "There are people who know what we can do and they seek to use us for a lot of different reasons. And others think we are dangerous and want to eradicate us from the Earth."

Ananda was a bit startled by the information. "Wait, why do some people think we're dangerous?" The question made Jared breathe deeply as he struggled with reawakened guilt from the past.

"There have been issues with those of us who struggle with the gift. Hearing voices isn't considered…normal I guess, and some of us can't handle it and lose touch with reality." Jared took a deep breath before deciding to be completely honest with the woman he wanted to be with. He knew that starting their relationship based on lies would only create more problems as time went on. "When I was in high school, there was a kid that everyone bullied. I knew he had the gift because I could hear his thoughts, dark thoughts about silencing the voices and I wanted…" Jared's breath shuttered as he tried hard not to let his feelings of his past overwhelm him. Ananda couldn't take her eyes off of Jared, a feeling of dismay filling her mind. She could feel the distress flowing off of the man in waves. Her comfort gave Jared the strength to continue.

"I wanted to tell him he wasn't alone, but I was terrified. I had only recently gotten control of my own ability and my parents weren't talking about sending me away for treatment anymore and I thought that if I said something, they would think I had a relapse. So I

stayed quiet; I didn't talk to the kid any more than
necessary and I didn't tell anyone what he was
thinking."

Ananda could feel herself horribly fascinated. It was
as if she could picture what happened in her mind's
eye. Somehow she saw the boy from Jared's story enter
into a cafeteria, intent on silencing the voices that
repeatedly tormented him. Looking around she saw
jocks laughing and pointing, their words cruel and
biting. She saw a table of girls throwing looks at the
young man, disgust clearly evident on their young
faces. And yet through it all, she could see one lone
figure, a girl with a cascade of dark hair, high cheek
bones and eyes of indescribable color and somehow she
knew, this girl was Jared's sister. Unbelievably, for a
moment the two girls' eyes connected and Ananda
knew that she was being seen as surely as she knew
what would happen next.

"Take care of him," the other girl whispered as
chaos erupted in the cafeteria and a jolt unlike one
Ananda had ever experienced pushed her consciousness
back into the present where Jared was worriedly staring
at her. She was unsurprised to find tears in her eyes as a
sob worked its way from her throat.

"I saw her Jared," Ananda whispered, throat raspy
with emotion. "I saw Sophie."

Though he had pledged to himself to keep Ananda
safe, he was unprepared for the effect her scent would
have on him. He found himself hardening fast, and even
though they were surrounded by the stench of trash and

waste, the desire to bend her over and have her right then and there was damn near overwhelming. Only the thought of being caught by whoever had been hunting him kept him from doing something incredibly stupid in the alley. No, he will save it for later.

In retrospect, being contained in a small space with the object of your desire spilling fresh pheromones everywhere probably wasn't the best idea he had ever had. If he had been a better man, he would have gotten two separate rooms and retreated to take care of his sexual frustration alone. He may have been able to control himself if not for the innocent thought that drifted his way.

"Why do you smell so good?"

The realization that Ananda could smell him as much as he could smell her broke whatever control Jared thought he had and before he could regain his senses he found himself balls deep, buried in a warmth that threatened to break the tenuous hold he had on his feelings. Every thrust felt like a cleansing and every gasp and moan like the words of an angel. Afterwards as he lay beside her sleeping body, Jared's eyes took in everything about her from the point of her nose to the ample swelling of her bosom. Somehow in the midst of so much chaos and pain, he had managed to find the woman who would complete him. He didn't know how he knew, but he just knew. And now that he had her wrapped safely in his arms, he dared anyone to try to come and rip them apart.

He knew that this battle wasn't over; it hadn't even truly begun. For some reason there were people out there hunting people like him and Ananda, and Jared would not rest until he could be sure that the woman asleep in his arms would be safe.

To be continued in Book 4

If you enjoyed this title, I would appreciate your leaving a review of the book. Good reviews encourage an author to write as well as help books to sell. Good reviews can be just a few short sentences describing what you liked about the book without having a spoiler. If you could spend 30 seconds writing a review, I would appreciate it: you can review this title right now at your favorite retailer.

Here is a preview of the **next story** you may enjoy:

Revealed - The Mind Talker Paranormal Romance Series, Book 4

JARED WAS quiet for the next few hours as they continued their drive. He hadn't responded when Ananda explained that she had seen his sister and the message she had given her. The idea that not only had Sophie known about her brother's gift but somehow also had the gift herself was alarming and Ananda just knew that asking questions now would be a bad move. So rather than talk and risk upsetting the man further, Ananda decided to catch up on as much sleep as possible. She was still unsure of their destination and secretly she was terrified that the dark figure from her vision would find them before they reached whatever destination they were heading to.

"I'm sorry." The sound of Jared's voice was almost overly loud in the quiet of the car. Ananda opened her eyes but refused to turn around. Somehow she knew that whatever the man needed to say, it would be much easier for him to get it out if she weren't looking at him. "I'm not angry with you…it's just…" Jared paused, as if to gather courage. "The whole time we were growing up, Sophie never ever told me she had a gift. Not even when I started hearing voices and told her. I always thought that if I had done more, I could have saved her that day. If only I had told someone about Kevin instead of hiding away like a coward. Or if I had stayed in the cafeteria that day…"

"Then you would have died along with everyone else and you wouldn't have been here, now, alive and able to keep me from being caught or killed by whoever is after me!" Ananda couldn't help but turn to look at the man. The sound of his grief was almost more than she could bear. "I didn't know your sister, but I'm sure she would never have wanted you to be there that day. She was your big sister and for some reason, for some reason that I just can't explain, I know she knew what was going to happen."

If not for his iron grip on the steering wheel, Jared might have jerked out of his chair with shock. "What?" He couldn't wrap his head around the thought. Even if Sophie had had the gift, she wasn't old enough for extra abilities to have manifested. "She wasn't old enough to have that ability. Abilities like that don't manifest until after maturation."

"I know, I know you said that but…I don't know how to explain it Jared." She put her hand softly on Jared's shoulder, willing him to understand what she saw and felt. Suddenly a tingling sensation manifested almost like an itch behind her ear. The feeling traveled down her arm and into the tips of her fingers as they rested against Jared's warm skin until she was sure that the man had to be feeling something. It was odd how surely Ananda felt about Jared when they had only met one another seventy-two hours ago. She spared a thought for Kerri and wondered what her dearest friend was doing in her absence. "Do you think I could call Kerri, or my parents? I mean, would it be safe to call them? They aren't in any danger right?"

If you enjoyed this sample then look for **Revealed - The Mind Talker Paranormal Romance Series, Book 4**.

Here is a preview of **another story** you may enjoy:

Forgotten - The Daemon Paranormal Romance Chronicles, Book 3

ROLLING OUT of bed, Phoebe looked on Supay's sleeping form. After spending several weeks with him in Puerto Rico, she decided to move back to Peru, where he lived for most of the year. Her life had taken a strange turn. Instead of working at her fortune telling shop, she was now essentially a kept woman. During the day, they worked together to stop the fighting that kept breaking out in the daemon world. The daemons were essentially a different type of human, and each daemon possessed a unique power. Phoebe could read minds, while Supay could transform into any animal. These unique abilities had given rise to the ancient mythologies of past years. In honor of their ancestors, Phoebe's daemon family had chosen to name all of their children after Greek gods and prophets.

Phoebe threw on a robe and turned on the shower. Over the last few months, she had learned that she was a daemon and that she still had a mother. Her mother, Rhea, had been raped and conceived twin girls. Her twin sister had never made it past birth, but Phoebe had been born. With her gift of mind-reading, she had been in constant pain as an infant because she could see her mother's memories of the rape. Traumatized by the rape and inability to touch her daughter, Rhea had placed Phoebe in foster care. Phoebe finally found out that she was a daemon and about the true story when Apollo came looking for help with killing the Qilin.

Stepping into the shower, Phoebe let the warm water drift along her body. The sensation was pleasant and woke her up. Today, she needed to go with Supay to meet a daemon called Juno. According to the reports, Juno was the daemon behind much of the infighting. With the death of the Qilin, a leader was supposed to appear that would bring peace. According to prophecy, it seemed like Apollo should have been that person. Since he was still brooding over beer about the loss of Phoebe and the killing of the Qilin, Supay had convinced Phoebe that they needed to take action together.

Phoebe heard the shower curtain open. Turning, she saw…

If you enjoyed this sample then look for **Forgotten - The Daemon Paranormal Romance Chronicles, Book 3**.

Here is a preview of **another story** you may enjoy:

Alpha Packed: A BBW Paranormal Shifter Romance - Book 3

IDRIS FLEXED his hand, wanting to rip off the bandage around his wrist. He knew what was under there and didn't care if it ever healed. But he was still too injured to do much of anything and ended up lying back down in bed. When Darlene finished work, she planned to come over to help take care of him. He found himself wanting to see her more than ever.

He had been foolish to even think about Vivica in a sexual manner again. He clearly took too long to give her the answer she had been looking for, because she made sure Roman got the fight that he wanted. She wanted Idris dead, all because he wouldn't go back into her twisted arms but chose Darlene instead.

Now Roman was dead. Idris was injured and still recovering. And he was an Exsul.

He stared at the bandage again. The tattoo was healing but it itched. Of all the pain and injustices he'd suffered recently, this was the worst.

Roman's pack lied and said Idris had started the fight even though Roman declined. The truth was that Vivica had led Idris right to the pack, and Roman had started the fight. Idris would have died if it hadn't been for the spirit that Darlene had sent to him, choking Roman and allowing him the upper hand.

He lived, but the packs voted to sentence him with Exsul status in an emergency meeting. As far as everyone knew and believed, Idris had killed Roman and defied pack law.

Now he was Exsul. Like Maria.

Like Attitcus, the man who had Changed him all those years ago.

For the first time in a long time, Idris felt lost. There was no pack, no rules to follow, just a lonely life ahead of him. He had Darlene, and he was happy he was with her, but he couldn't shake the fact that she wasn't a werewolf. At full moons, he'd have to run alone in the woods. He would have no voice in anything that determined the future of packs or laws. He would never read *The Werewolf Code* again.

Out of all the injuries on his body, the one that ached the most was the tattoo. It represented much more than an injury from Roman. It represented the loss of everything he knew and held dear.

Darlene checked over her shoulder before getting into her car. It had become a habit since taking Rosamund's herbs to help her connect with her spirit powers. She hadn't seen the ghost of Lucian since the night he lured her to Rebecca, but she still worried she'd see him again. She was also terrified that she would see Rebecca as well. How do you talk to the ghost of the vampire you had to stake? Especially when Darlene felt responsible for turning her into both.

Her phone blinked... a missed call from the police station. They had follow-up questions for her about Officer Walsh, but Darlene played dumb on every aspect. The new person in charge of the case, Detective Curry, seemed a lot lazier than Walsh. She was banking on that laziness and hoping he'd lose interest in questioning her after this. Rebecca had killed Walsh, in a misguided attempt to get the heat off of Darlene and show her how much she valued their friendship.

Darlene shook her head, trying to clear her mind of past ghosts. She had enough to deal with. Trying to figure out her own powers was a handful as it was. Rosamund's herbs had broken down whatever mental block she had, but sometimes fear clogged her from seeing everything. Sometimes her excitement meant she saw too many spirits at once. She had a follow-up appointment to see Rosamund tomorrow night but was secretly dreading it. Rosamund's house smelled weird, and she talked in strange riddles.

But Rosamund was the only one who knew about this sort of thing. And her herbs helped. Darlene just didn't know how to properly control it.

But tonight she had bigger things to focus on. She was going over to see Idris in his hotel room, which he had stayed in for over a month now. Darlene wasn't sure where he was going to go – now that he was Exsul. He had no pack to run with and nowhere to stay. Darlene had suggested he talk to Maria about it, but that only made him furious.

She knew that Vivica had a hand in setting up the confrontation between Roman and Idris, all because he wouldn't jump back to her. Vivica had the chance to kill her as well, but didn't. Darlene figured it was because she was so sure that Idris was dead, she didn't feel like killing her after Darlene had killed Rebecca.

Darlene knew nothing about Vivica other than that she was an ancient vampire with a deadly love for Idris.

Now Roman was dead, Mark was pack leader and Idris was Exsul. Not to mention hybrid Jacob was still out there somewhere. The whole thing made her head hurt.

Darlene drove out of the bookstore parking lot. Business had slowed a little since they reopened. Darlene was eager for it to go back to how it used to be – barely any customers and a big sale about once a month. That was what she preferred.

It didn't take long to make it to Idris's hotel room. The moon was high in the sky by the time she got there. She hated walking around at night, terrified that at any moment a vampire or something else would snatch her. Darlene had technically been kidnapped twice now and was completely over it.

She knocked on the hotel room door, and Idris called for her to come in. Darlene stepped inside. He was propped up in bed, watching the nightly news. He looked like shit, although she wasn't going to point it out.

"Hey. How are you feeling?"

"Great," he mumbled.

Once Exsul status was given and Idris's condition was stabilized, he had to leave pack headquarters. Darlene took care of him here the best that she could. He healed quickly because he was a werewolf and was almost fully recovered. She figured the reason that Idris dragged his heels about getting out of bed was because he was depressed.

"How was work?" he asked as she sat on the bed next to him.

She shrugged. "Same old. Nothing exciting."

Idris lapsed into silence. Darlene chewed on her bottom lip, unsure of what to say. Trying to get through to Idris was like trying to get a rock to talk. She wasn't even sure if he enjoyed her company. He refused to talk about his new status, although his hand kept tugging on the bandage around the tattoo that marked him as Exsul.

"Are you coming over tomorrow night?"

"I have to work till close," she lied.

Even though Idris had no pack now, Rosamund had strictly forbidden Darlene from telling him that Darlene was seeing her. She wasn't sure why, and Rosamund refused to tell. Maria didn't know either. She told Darlene that the only reason Rosamund would see her was because she was Exsul. Idris still had too many close ties to Liara's pack. Darlene didn't like lying about seeing a witch, but she didn't want to piss anyone off either.

Idris merely grunted in reply, not questioning anything. Darlene wasn't even sure if he was listening. She felt frustration build up inside her chest but told herself to stop. She couldn't imagine what he was going through – and she blamed herself for it.

She blamed herself for everything these days.

The hotel room was silent. Idris had his eyes closed and the TV muted. Colors danced against his eyelids. Darlene had left an hour ago, around ten. She usually stayed the night, but he knew why she lied and said she had to get home. He was terrible company and he knew it, especially tonight. He just didn't know how to change it. He didn't know how to ask for help either.

He didn't know anything anymore.

Liara's face swam into view when she delivered the news of his Exsul status.

"You know this is bullshit," Idris growled, barely awake in the hospital bed at pack headquarters.

"Roman is dead, Idris. The packs have voted. It is out of my hands."

In that moment, he hated her. It was irrational and stupid. She had done nothing wrong. As pack leader, she had followed the rules, even when he knew that her heart was still breaking over what Lucian had done. And he had made it even worse, in a fit of rage, when he told her that Lucian had been involved with Vivica.

"Why are you telling me this now?" she asked, staring down at him in the bed.

Because I'm furious, and I'm taking it out on you.

"Because you should know Lucian was cheating on you emotionally, at the very least," he said instead.

Liara left, and he knew he had made her cry. He was becoming someone he didn't even like.

There was a soft knock on the door, bringing Idris back to the present. He opened his eyes, frowning. If it was Vivica, he would stake her right now. He wouldn't even hesitate. His blood started to pump and he slid out of bed, looking for something to stake her with. The knocking came again, harder this time. He would just Change and lunge, he decided, as he slowly walked over to the door. He opened the door, ready to lash out at Vivica.

But he was stopped cold by the man in his doorway. Older, with crooked glasses and gray hair. Lines around his face and eyes. Slightly hunched over. Clothes too big for him.

"Idris," the man said, making Idris's blood run cold. "Heard you're one of us now."

The man pulled up his sleeve, exposing his Exsul tattoo. Idris's head began to pound, like an explosion going off in his brain.

This man had ruined his life and left him out to dry.

"Atticus," Idris breathed.

If you enjoyed this sample then look for **Alpha Packed: A BBW Paranormal Shifter Romance - Book 3.**

Other Books by Darla Dunbar

- The Romeo Alpha BBW Paranormal Shifter Romance Series

- Romeo Alpha Blood Lines Romance Series

- The Alpha Feud BBW Paranormal Shifter Romance Series

- The Alpha Packed BBW Paranormal Shifter Romance Series

- The Daemon Paranormal Romance Chronicles

- The Leather Satchel Paranormal Romance Series

Get the latest update on new releases from the author at:

https://darladunbar.com/newsletter/

About the Author - Darla Dunbar

Darla has been interested in paranormal romance since she was a teenager in high school. It was then that she discovered she could fulfill her fantasies through her writing.

Observing people and human behavior in the area of romance has always been one of her favorite pastimes. Combining that with an overactive imagination is a sure fire way of coming up with interesting themes.

Connect with Darla Dunbar

I really appreciate you reading my book! Here are my social media coordinates:

Friend me on Facebook:
https://www.facebook.com/darladunbar/

Follow me on Twitter: https://twitter.com/DarlDunbar

Check me out on Goodreads:
https://www.goodreads.com/author/show/8425857.Darl a_Dunbar

Subscribe to my newsletter:
https://darladunbar.com/newsletter/

Visit my website: https://darladunbar.com/

www.ingramcontent.com/pod-product-compliance
Lightning Source LLC
Chambersburg PA
CBHW030825200726
48288CB00004B/1398